ABOVE THE RIM

THE NBA LIBRARY

CENTRAL DIVISION

BY ROBERT E.
SCHNAKENBERG

THE ATLANTA HAWKS
THE CHICAGO BULLS
THE CLEVELAND CAVALIERS
THE DETROIT PISTONS
THE INDIANA PACERS
THE MILWAUKEE BUCKS
THE NEW ORLEANS HORNETS
THE TORONTO RAPTORS

THE CENTRAL DIVISION: The Atlanta Hawks, the Chicago Bulls, the Cleveland Cavaliers, the Detroit Pistons, the Indiana Pacers, the Milwaukee Bucks, the New Orleans Hornets, and the Toronto Raptors

Published in the United States of America by The Child's World®
PO Box 326 • Chanhassen, MN 55317-0326 • 800-599-READ • www.childsworld.com

ACKNOWLEDGEMENTS:
The Child's World®: Mary Berendes, Publishing Director

Editorial Directions, Inc.: E. Russell Primm, Editorial Director and Line Editor; Katie Marsico, Assistant Editor; Matthew Messbarger, Editorial Assistant; Susan Hindman, Copy Editor; Melissa McDaniel, Proofreader; Tim Griffin, Indexer; Kevin Cunningham, Fact Checker; James Buckley Jr., Photo Reseacher and Photo Selector

The Design Lab: Kathleen Petelinsek, Designer and Production Artist

PHOTOS:
Cover: AP/Wide World.
AP/Wide World: 4, 7, 10, 14, 18, 23, 26, 28, 36, 37, 39, 40, 41, 44.
AFP/Corbis: 25.
Bettmann/Corbis: 8, 20, 30.
Sports Gallery: 9, 12, 13, 16, 17, 21, 22, 27, 31, 34, 35.

LIBRARY OF CONGRESS CATALOGING-IN-PUBLICATION DATA
Cataloging-in-Publication data for this title has been applied for and is available from the United States Library of Congress.

Note to readers: At press time, the NBA was considering a plan that would reorganize the league into six divisions of five teams, beginning in the 2004-05 season. It will also add a 30th team, the Charlotte Bobcats.

The Central Division of the National Basketball Association (NBA) is a mix of old and new. Some teams date back to the early days of the NBA, like the Detroit Pistons. Others, such as the Chicago Bulls, entered the league in the 1960s. Still others have been in existence for only a few years, like the Toronto Raptors. It's a division of great old rivalries and new, emerging ones.

Six of the eight teams in the Central have played together in that division since 1980. The Hornets joined the party in 1988 and the Raptors in 1995. A number of teams have switched cities—in some cases

Michael Jordan and the Bulls captured six NBA titles in the 1990s.

more than once. The Atlanta Hawks, for example, have played in Milwaukee, St. Louis, and Atlanta—not to mention three different cities in Illinois and Iowa! Three of the Central Division teams started out in other leagues before joining the NBA. It's tough sorting out all these comings and goings, but we'll try.

One thing is for sure: the Central Division has been home to some great basketball. Central teams have accounted for 10 NBA championships. The division has featured some of the game's legendary players, such as Michael Jordan and Kareem Abdul-Jabbar. Younger stars such as Vince Carter have tried to build on this tradition of excellence. Read on to learn about this exciting division's past—and future.

TEAM	YEAR FOUNDED	HOME ARENA	YEAR ARENA OPENED	TEAM COLORS
ATLANTA HAWKS	1946	PHILIPS ARENA	1999	RED, BLACK, & YELLOW
CHICAGO BULLS	1966	UNITED CENTER	1994	RED & BLACK
CLEVELAND CAVALIERS	1970	GUND ARENA	1994	WINE & GOLD
DETROIT PISTONS	1941	THE PALACE OF AUBURN HILLS	1988	RED, YELLOW, GREEN, SILVER & BLACK
INDIANA PACERS	1967	CONSECO FIELDHOUSE	1999	NAVY BLUE & GOLD
MILWAUKEE BUCKS	1968	BRADLEY CENTER	1988	GREEN, PURPLE, & SILVER
NEW ORLEANS HORNETS	1988	NEW ORLEANS ARENA	1999	TEAL, PURPLE, & WHITE
TORONTO RAPTORS	1995	AIR CANADA CENTRE	1999	RED, PURPLE, BLACK & SILVER

THE ATLANTA HAWKS

The Atlanta Hawks are one of the NBA's oldest and most historic franchises. That might surprise some people, because the team has only been playing in its current home city since 1968. But the Hawks' basketball tradition stretches back much further than that.

From 1946 to 1951, the team was known as the Tri-City Blackhawks. They played in the old National Basketball League (NBL). In 1949, the NBL merged with another league to form the NBA. One of the team's coaches in these early days was Arnold "Red" Auerbach, who later became the coach of the Boston Celtics.

In 1951, the Blackhawks moved to Milwaukee and shortened their name to the Hawks. Just four years later, they moved again—this time to Saint Louis. The Saint Louis Hawks made the **NBA Finals** in 1957, 1958, 1960, and 1961. In 1958, they won it all, defeating Auerbach's Celtics in six games.

Bob Pettit soared for the Hawks in the 1950s.

Leading the Hawks during this period was Bob Pettit, a talented scorer who spent his entire career with the team.

In 1968, the Hawks shocked their fans again by moving to Atlanta. The modern era of Hawks basketball had begun. The 1970s was an up-and-down decade for the franchise. Highly successful seasons were often followed by disastrous ones. In 1977, millionaire broadcaster Ted Turner bought the team. He helped bring consistency back to the

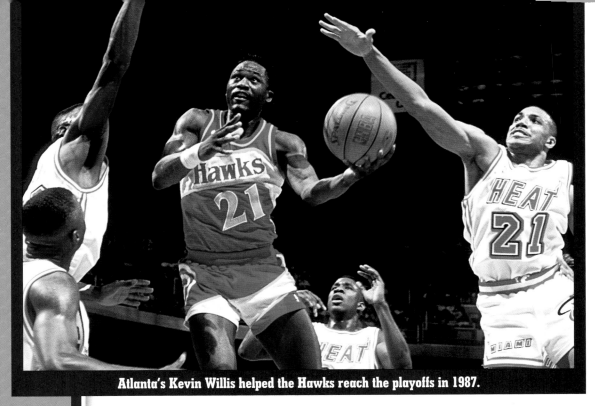

Atlanta's Kevin Willis helped the Hawks reach the playoffs in 1987.

Hawks, laying the groundwork for Central Division titles in 1980 and 1987.

Turner's biggest move came in 1982, when he traded two players to Utah for the rights to Dominique Wilkins, a former **All-American** player at the University of Georgia. Wilkins led the Hawks through the 1980s. He became the team's all-time champion in both scoring and steals. While the Hawks never won an NBA title during this period, they were one of the league's most entertaining teams.

That trend continued in the 1990s. The Hawks made the **playoffs** nine straight seasons, capturing the

Four on one? No problem for the high-flying Dominique Wilkins.

Central Division crown in 1994. Key players
during this run included Wilkins (who was traded in
1995), center Dikembe Mutombo, and **backcourt** man
Steve Smith. In recent years, the Hawks have begun
building their team around younger players like
Jason Terry and Shareef Abdur-Rahim. Given the
eventful history of this franchise, it seems like just a
matter of time before the Hawks are flying again.

Forward Sharif Abdur-Rahim is the hottest young Hawks talent.

THE CHICAGO BULLS

When people think of the Chicago Bulls, they immediately think of Michael Jordan. But while "Air Jordan" is the most important figure in Bulls history, he's not the only one. The Bulls have been entertaining fans in the Windy City for nearly four decades.

The Bulls began play in 1966. The new squad quickly won the city over by posting the best record ever for an **expansion** team, 33–48. It was even good enough to make the playoffs, where the Bulls were eliminated by the St. Louis Hawks.

The Bulls did not build on that early success until the 1970s, however. That's when a new group of players led by Bob Love and Norm Van Lier led the team to four straight 50-win seasons and a regular spot in the NBA playoffs. Defensive specialist Jerry Sloan, one of the original expansion Bulls, was also a standout in this period. His hard-nosed play helped Chicago capture a division title in 1975.

Forward Scottie Pippen and coach Phil Jackson were vital parts of the Bulls' six titles.

Injuries and the retirement of key players ended the Bulls' competitive run, however. The team slid into a long period of mediocrity. That began to end when Michael Jordan joined the team in 1984. The athletic guard out of the University of North Carolina made an immediate impact on the franchise. He won the NBA Rookie of the Year award and emerged as one of the NBA's top scorers. But Jordan's high-flying dunks weren't enough to make the Bulls a contender. The team had to add other good players around him. Important **role players** such as Scottie Pippen and Horace Grant helped

Air Jordan soars! The most famous number
in basketball was Michael Jordan's 23.

Michael Jordan and Phil Jackson with the Bulls' 1998 NBA championship trophies.

Chicago capture the Central Division crown in 1991. The Bulls capped that season by defeating the Lakers in five games to win Chicago's first NBA title.

Additional championships followed in 1992, 1993, 1996, 1997, and 1998. Long considered a laughingstock, the Bulls were now the standard by which other teams measured themselves. Jordan joined the ranks of the all-time greats. His retirement in 1998 ended one of the most successful runs of any team in sports history. Since he left town, the Bulls have struggled to develop a new identity as a team. The passion Chicagoans showed for the team during its championship days ensures that it's only a matter of time before "Da Bulls" are playing before packed houses again.

Bulls owner Jerry Reinsdorf also owns Major League Baseball's Chicago White Sox.

CHAPTER 3

THE CLEVELAND CAVALIERS

The Cleveland Cavaliers seem to specialize in heartbreaking defeats. Like baseball's Chicago Cubs, they climb out from the bottom of the standings every few years, only to tumble back down again once they get close to success. If nothing else, these ups and downs have made them interesting to watch.

The Cavaliers joined the NBA in 1970. It was not a promising beginning. The team went 15–67 and played in a half-empty arena. About the only thing the team had going for it was coach Bill Fitch's sense of humor. "I phoned Dial-a-Prayer," Fitch said during one bad losing streak, "but when they found out who it was, they hung up."

It took a long time, but Cleveland's prayers were finally answered. Led by center Nate Thurmond, the team enjoyed its first winning season in 1975–76. They captured the Central Division title and made it all the way to the Eastern Conference Finals. There Fitch and his crew suf-

Mark Price's dribbling skills were key to Cleveland's success.

The Cavaliers' home court, Gund Arena, is the only one in the NBA named after a team owner—businessman Gordon Gund.

fered the first of many heartbreaks, falling to the Boston Celtics in six games.

From 1978 to 1987, Cleveland fielded consistently poor teams, never winning more games than it lost. Things began to improve in the late 1980s. The team drafted talented young players like Brad Daugherty, Ron Harper, and Mark Price. No matter how good the team got, however, it could not seem to get past the Chicago Bulls, led by Michael

Brad Daugherty pointed the way to the playoffs for the Cavaliers.

LeBron James figures to be the NBA's next young superstar.

The team's name was chosen by the fans as part of a newspaper contest. A cavalier is a soldier mounted on a horse.

In 2003, the Cavaliers announced a return to the team's original uniform colors—wine and gold. They had switched to orange and blue in 1983.

Jordan. In 1989, Jordan's **jumper** at the buzzer sent the excellent Cavs squad home early from the play-offs. A few years later, in 1993, he did it again. The Cavs also fell to the Bulls in the 1992 Eastern Conference Finals.

After these shattering defeats, the Cavaliers began the long process of **rebuilding.** They used the draft and signed foreign-born players like center Zydrunas Ilgauskus in an attempt to return to playoff contention. The biggest news in Cleveland in a decade came when the Cavs drafted LeBron James in 2003. Only 18, the multi-talented James quickly became one of the NBA's most popular players.

THE DETROIT PISTONS

One of the NBA's oldest franchises, the Detroit Pistons never won a championship until the arrival of Isiah Thomas and his "Bad Boys" of the late 1980s. After a rebuilding period, the team has recently shown signs of a return to glory.

The Pistons were founded in 1941 by an automobile piston maker named Fred Zollner. He based his team in Fort Wayne, Indiana, and called it the Fort Wayne Zollner Pistons. After several years in the NBL, the club joined the NBA's Central Division in 1949. They made the NBA Finals in 1955 and 1956, losing both times. The Pistons then fell on hard times, becoming one of the NBA's worst teams.

Relocated to Detroit, Michigan, in 1957, the Pistons cracked the .500 mark only three times from 1957 through 1983. Their best years came in the mid-1970s, when they were led by the talented inside-outside tandem of guard Dave Bing and cen-

Bob Lanier used his long reach to set scoring records.

ter Bob Lanier. In 1980, the franchise bottomed
out, winning only 16 of 82 games. The only good
thing about the Pistons' poor play was that it
allowed the team to get high draft picks. The team
used these to draft the backcourt duo of Isiah
Thomas and Joe Dumars. Detroit also traded wisely,
picking up **big man** Bill Laimbeer and other important role players.

In 1989, all this wheeling and dealing paid off.
The Pistons won 63 games—a franchise record—and

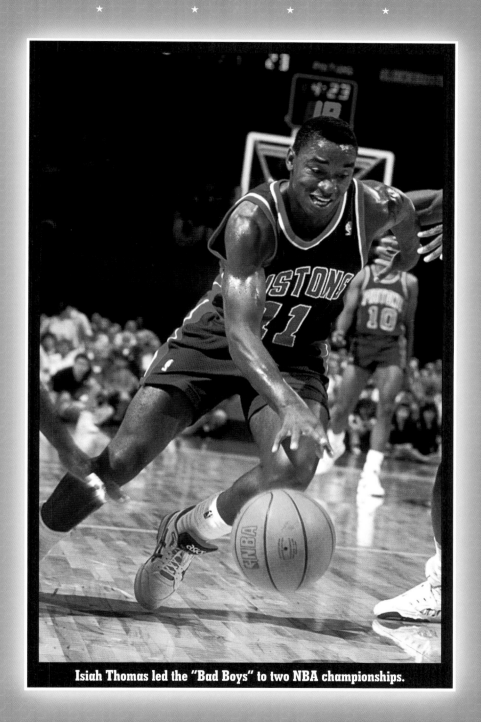

Isiah Thomas led the "Bad Boys" to two NBA championships.

Grant Hill was a top scorer for Detroit.

the team's first-ever
NBA title. Led by
coach Chuck Daly,
the club employed a
bruising defense that
earned it the nick-
name Bad Boys. The
Bad Boys were even
badder in 1990,
stomping the Port-
land Trail Blazers in
five games for the
back-to-back champi-
onship.

  After these glory
years, age caught up
with some of the
Pistons' best players.
The franchise
regained a great deal
of its energy in the
1990s with the arrival
of Grant Hill, a
dynamic forward out

Ben Wallace of Detroit has twice been named
the NBA's top defensive player.

Another larger-
than-life 1980s
Piston was Dennis
"Worm" Rodman.
The colorful
rebounding special-
ist later racked up
three more NBA
titles with the
Chicago Bulls.

of Duke University. In 2002, the retooled Pistons
surprised many NBA observers by capturing the
Central Division title. To do so, they employed a
defensive style that reminded longtime fans of the
champions of the past. The Bad Boys were back in
the driver's seat in the Motor City.

The NBA Western
Conference champi-
onship trophy is
named in honor of
Pistons founder
Fred Zollner.

THE INDIANA PACERS

Basketball is big in Indiana. The Hoosier State's passionate fans have rooted hard for their hometown Pacers since 1967. They have witnessed some terrific basketball and come "this close" to seeing their team win an NBA championship.

From 1967 to 1976, the Pacers played in the old American Basketball Association (ABA). The league was known for its freewheeling style of play and the use of red-white-and-blue basketballs. The Pacers won the ABA title three times and drew large and enthusiastic crowds. When the ABA merged with the NBA in 1976, the popular Pacers were invited to join the enlarged league.

At first, Indiana struggled in the NBA. In their first 13 seasons, they posted only one winning record. Fans still came out to cheer them on, however. Stars from this period included Billy Knight and George McGinnis. The Pacers joined the NBA Central Division in 1979.

Coach Larry Bird shows star Reggie Miller the way to go.

In the late 1980s, Pacer fortunes improved. The team added sharpshooting forward Chuck Person, known as "the Rifleman," and a talented center from Holland, Rik Smits. The team's most important young player was guard Reggie Miller from University of California, Los Angeles (UCLA). He became one of the league's best **clutch shooters**. With this **nucleus** of players, the Pacers stormed into playoff contention. In 1994, 1995, and 1998, the team made it all the way to the Eastern

The Pacers were named after the pace car used in the running of the hometown Indianapolis 500.

Dutchman Rik Smits was a towering force, both rebounding and scoring.

Former Pacer
forward Way-
man Tisdale is
now a successful
jazz guitarist.

Conference Finals. Though they lost all three times, Miller's heart-stopping last-second shots excited Pacer fans and made them feel an NBA title was just around the corner. The team even hired Indiana basketball legend Larry Bird as coach in 1997 to make that dream a reality.

In 2000, the Pacers finally got their big chance. The team faced the Los Angeles Lakers in the NBA Finals. The Lakers, led by Shaquille O'Neal, were heavily favored. But the tough-minded Pacers would

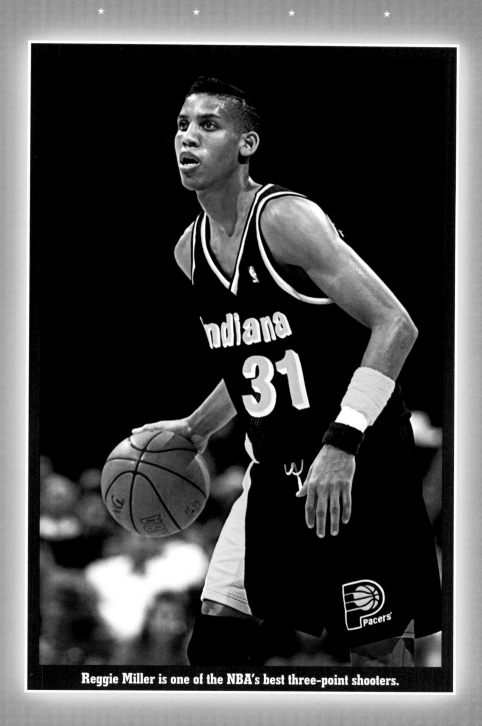

Reggie Miller is one of the NBA's best three-point shooters.

not go down easy. They fought the Lakers through five games before losing in the sixth, 116–111.

It was a tough loss to take. Some said the Pacers were now too old to compete for an NBA title. However, the club immediately began rebuilding for the future. Former Celtics star and Pacers coach Larry Bird became the club president in 2003. Forwards Jermaine O'Neal and Ron Artest joined Miller in the Pacers' quest to return to the playoffs.

Powerful Ron Artest of the Pacers is tough for opponents to defend.

THE MILWAUKEE BUCKS

The Milwaukee Bucks got off to a record-breaking start. They won a league championship faster than any team in sports history. While there have been some lean years since then, for the most part the Bucks have been consistent winners since they joined the NBA in 1968.

The Bucks can thank a lucky coin toss for their early success. In 1969, the team won the toss to determine who picked first in the NBA draft. They selected UCLA center Lew Alcindor, who would later change his name to Kareem Abdul-Jabbar. He led the Bucks to the conference title in his rookie season. The next year, the graceful big man helped Milwaukee win the NBA title. He spent six seasons in Milwaukee and was named the NBA's Most Valuable Player in 1971, 1972, and 1974.

The other star player with the Bucks at this time was Oscar Robertson. Nicknamed "the Big O," Robertson was a veteran **point guard** who excelled at making tough passes. The teamwork between these

The man they called "The Big O" was perhaps the best all-around player of the 1960s.

two future Hall of Famers made the early 1970s a golden era for Bucks basketball.

After Robertson retired and Abdul-Jabbar moved on to Los Angeles, the Bucks struggled. They did not win 50 games in a season again until 1981. They won the Central Division that year and the next five years in a row. In fact, the Bucks enjoyed 12 straight winning seasons from 1979–80 through 1990–91. But the team never could make it back to the NBA Finals.

Kareem Abdul-Jabbar helped the Bucks
win their only NBA title in 1971.

Milwaukee native Terry Porter took over as the Bucks' coach in 2003.

Former Buck Ray
Allen is also a
movie actor. He
starred with Denzel
Washington in the
1998 basketball
drama *He Got
Game.*

In the 1990s, the Bucks went into a period of
decline. Many thought the arrival of forward Glenn
"Big Dog" Robinson would reverse their fortunes,
but it was not to be.

The club did not return to the top of the
Central Division until 2001. Perhaps the "luck of
the Bucks" that helped them get so good so quickly
was finally beginning to turn around!

THE NEW ORLEANS HORNETS

The Hornets began playing in a state best known for its college basketball tradition and moved to a city famous for jazz music. Wherever they've played, they have brought youthful excitement and won over many new fans.

The NBA thought Charlotte would be a great place to put an expansion team in 1988. North Carolina was known for its passionate basketball fans, who followed hometown college teams like Duke and Wake Forest. Many of those same fans filled the Charlotte Arena, known as the Hive, to see NBA play. The Hornets fed off that enthusiasm for 13 seasons in the Tar Heel state.

A number of those early Hornets became fan favorites. Point guard Tyrone "Muggsy" Bogues was only 5-foot-3, but he played with tremendous energy and competitive fire. Larry Johnson was drafted out of the University of Nevada–Las Vegas in 1991. "LJ" became the team's leader and

Muggsy Bogues was short in height, but long in talent.

Muggsy's best friend. In 1992, the team added Georgetown center Alonzo Mourning to its roster. Now the squad was complete. With Mourning's defense and rebounding setting the tone, the club made the playoffs in 1993. There they shocked the Boston Celtics, beating them in four games. The home fans went wild as Mourning's **buzzer-beater** sealed the victory.

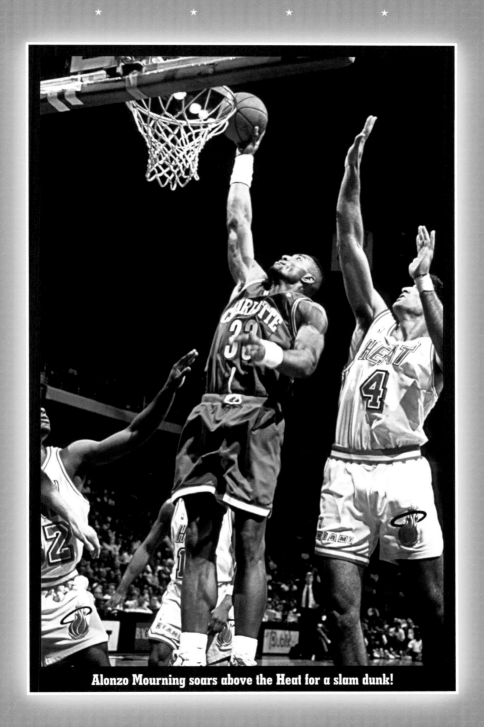

Alonzo Mourning soars above the Heat for a slam dunk!

Charlotte's Glen Rice was the 1997 All-Star Game MVP.

The young team continued to grow. The Hornets made the playoffs again in 1995. In 1996, they said goodbye to Johnson and Mourning in a pair of trades that shocked and angered many fans. The team managed to win back the crowds the following season, however. New Hornets Glen Rice and Vlade Divac led the team to a franchise record 54 victories. The Hive was buzzing again.

There were more changes to come. The team traded Bogues to Golden State in 1997. Players were saddened by the death of guard Bobby Phills in a car accident in 2000. But the biggest change of all came in 2002, when the team announced it would be moving to New Orleans for the 2002–03 season. The former home of the New Orleans Jazz welcomed its new team with open arms. The Hive may be gone, but the buzz around this team seems to be getting louder!

Jamal Mashburn was the high scorer for the Hornets in their new home.

THE TORONTO RAPTORS

The city of Toronto, Canada, waited almost 50 years for the return of professional basketball. Since 1995, the fast-rising Raptors have made its happy hoops fans wonder why they had to wait so long.

The Raptors may be only a few years old, but basketball in Toronto goes back to 1946. That's when the Toronto Huskies played their one and only season in the old Basketball Association of America. In 1993, the NBA announced that basketball would return to Toronto. It granted the city an expansion team, set to begin play in the 1995–96 season.

Toronto fans entered a contest to choose the team's name and colors. The winning name was Raptors, after a dinosaur in the movie *Jurassic Park*. Isiah Thomas, the retired point guard from the Detroit Pistons, was put in charge of building the team roster. Canadian fans hungry for NBA basketball snapped up season tickets at a rapid rate.

Marcus Camby posed with NBA commissioner David Stern after being chosen in the 1996 NBA Draft.

Like any expansion team, the Raptors struggled at first. Fans were patient, however, and they enjoyed watching young stars like Damon Stoudamire and Marcus Camby grow and improve. In 1999, another young Raptor, Vince Carter, won the Rookie of the Year award. The future looked bright.

The 1999–2000 season held several firsts for Toronto. Carter, nicknamed Air Canada, became the first Raptor to appear in an NBA All-Star Game. His high-flying dunks helped lead the team

Besides the Raptors, other names considered for the Toronto expansion team were the Beavers, the Bobcats, the Dragons, and the Grizzlies.

Vince Carter is one of the NBA's most electrifying dunkers.

The Raptors and Knicks played in the first-ever NBA playoff game in Canada in 2000.

into the playoffs for the first time as well. The
Raptors lost the first-ever **postseason** game played in
Canada to the New York Knicks to close out an
exciting series.

Toronto made the playoffs in each of the next
two seasons. In 2001, the Raptors even won a series,
beating the mighty New York Knicks 3–2. Carter was
hailed as one of the NBA's rising stars and the
Raptors one of its up-and-coming teams. The future,
like the past, looks bright for NBA action in Toronto.

The Raptors played
their first two sea-
sons in Toronto's
SkyDome, home to
baseball's Blue Jays.

TEAM RECORDS

TEAM	ALL-TIME RECORD	NBA TITLES (MOST RECENT)	NUMBER OF TIMES IN PLAYOFFS	TOP COACH (WINS)
ATLANTA	2142–2114	1 (1957–1958)	35	RICHIE GUERIN (327)
CHICAGO	1543–1458	6 (1997–1998)	24	PHIL JACKSON (545)
CLEVELAND	1172–1502	0	12	LENNY WILKENS (316)
DETROIT	2077–2241	2 (1989–1990)	34	CHUCK DALY (467)
INDIANA	1054–1128	0	15	BOB LEONARD (529)
MILWAUKEE	1545–1293	1 (1970–1971)	22	DON NELSON (540)
NEW ORLEANS	589–609	0	8	ALLAN BRISTOW (207)
TORONTO	248–376	0	3	LENNY WILKENS (188)

NBA CENTRAL CAREER LEADERS (THROUGH 2002–03)

TEAM	CATEGORY	NAME (YEARS WITH TEAM)	TOTAL
ATLANTA	POINTS	DOMINIQUE WILKINS (1982–1994)	23,292
	REBOUNDS	KEVIN WILLIS (1984–1994)	7,256
CHICAGO	POINTS	MICHAEL JORDAN (1984–1993) (1994–1998)	29,277
	REBOUNDS	MICHAEL JORDAN (1984–1993) (1994–1998)	5,836
CLEVELAND	POINTS	BRAD DAUGHERTY (1986–1996)	10,389
	REBOUNDS	BRAD DAUGHERTY (1986–1996)	5,227
DETROIT	POINTS	ISIAH THOMAS (1981–1994)	
	REBOUNDS	BILL LAIMBEER (1982–PRESENT)	9,430
INDIANA	POINTS	REGGIE MILLER (1987–PRESENT)	22,623
	REBOUNDS	MEL DANIELS (1968–1974)	7,643
MILWAUKEE	POINTS	KAREEM ABDUL-JABBAR (1969–1975)	14,211
	REBOUNDS	KAREEM ABDUL-JABBAR (1969–1975)	5,227
NEW ORLEANS	POINTS	DELL CURRY (1988–1998)	9,839
	REBOUNDS	LARRY JOHNSON (1991–1995)	3,479
TORONTO	POINTS	VINCE CARTER (1998–PRESENT)	7,458
	REBOUNDS	ANTONIO DAVIS (1999–PRESENT)	2,660

MEMBERS OF THE NAISMITH MEMORIAL NATIONAL BASKETBALL HALL OF FAME

ATLANTA

PLAYER	POSITION	DATE INDUCTED
Red Auerbach	Coach	1969
Walt Bellamy	Center	1993
Harry "the Horse" Gallatin	Coach	1991
Clifford Hagan	Guard/Forward	1978
Alex Hannum	Coach	1998
Connie Hawkins	Guard	1992
Red Holzman	Coach	1986
Bob Houbregs	Forward/Center	1987
Clyde Lovellette	Center	1988
Bobby McDermott	Guard	1988
Ed Macauley	Forward/Center	1960
Moses Malone	Center	2001
Pete Maravich	Guard	1987
Slater "Dugie" Martin	Guard	1982
Bob Pettit	Center	1971
Andy Phillip	Coach	1961
Lenny Wilkens	Guard/Coach	1989

CHICAGO

PLAYER	POSITION	DATE INDUCTED
George Gervin	Guard	1996
Nate Thurmond	Center	1985

CLEVELAND

PLAYER	POSITION	DATE INDUCTED
Chuck Daly	Coach	1994
Walt "Clyde" Frazier	Guard	1987
Harry "the Horse" Gallatin	Forward	1991
Nate Thurmond	Center	1985
Lenny Wilkens	Guard/Coach	1989

DETROIT

PLAYER	POSITION	DATE INDUCTED
Walt Bellamy	Center	1993
Dave Bing	Guard	1990
Chuck Daly	Coach	1994
Dave DeBusschere	Forward	1983
Bob Houbregs	Forward/Center	1987
Bailey Howell	Forward	1997
Harry "Buddy" Jeannette	Guard	1994
Bob Lanier	Center	1992
Bob McAdoo	Forward	2000
Bobby McDermott	Guard	1988
Dick McGuire	Guard	1993
Andy Phillip	Guard	1961
Isiah Thomas	Guard	2000
George Yardley	Forward	1996
Fred Zollner	Owner	1999

MEMBERS OF THE NAISMITH MEMORIAL NATIONAL BASKETBALL HALL OF FAME

Lenny Wilkens is the NBA's all-time winningest coach.

INDIANA

PLAYER	POSITION	DATE INDUCTED
Larry Brown	Coach	2002
Alex English	Forward	1997
Jack Ramsay	Coach	1992
Isiah Thomas	Coach	2000

MILWAUKEE

PLAYER	POSITION	DATE INDUCTED
Kareem Abdul-Jabbar	Center	1995
Nate "Tiny" Archibald	Guard	1991
Dave Cowens	Center	1991
Alex English	Forward	1997
Bob Lanier	Center	1992
Moses Malone	Center	2001
Oscar Robertson	Guard	1980

TORONTO

PLAYER	POSITION	DATE INDUCTED
Lenny Wilkens	Guard/Coach	1989

Note: New Orleans does not have any members of the Hall of Fame (yet!).

GLOSSARY

All-American—a player who has been selected as one of the best at his position by an organization or publication

backcourt—the area on a basketball court from the centerline to the baseline that a team defends

big man—another word for center

buzzer-beater—a successful last-second shot

clutch shooters—players who are skilled at making especially long or difficult shots

expansion—enlarging the league to admit new teams; expansion teams often struggle in their first few seasons

jumper—a shot in which a player jumps into the air and releases the ball from above his head; also called a jump shot

NBA Finals—a seven-game series between the winners of the NBA's Eastern and Western Conference championships

nucleus—the core group of players around which a team is built

playoffs—a four level post season elimination tournament involving eight teams for each conference; levels include two rounds of divisional playoffs (best of five games and best of seven), a conference championship round (best of seven), and the NBA Finals (best of seven)

point guard—the player who brings the ball upcourt for the offensive team

postseason—another name for the playoffs; a team must make it through three rounds to reach the NBA Finals

rebuilding—the process of building a team back up again after a period of poor play

role players—players who specialize in one or two aspects of the game, such as defense or rebounding

TIME LINE

1941 The Pistons are founded as the Fort Wayne Zollner Pistons

1946 The Hawks are founded as the Tri-City Blackhawks

1958 The Saint Louis Hawks win the NBA title

1966 The Chicago Bulls are founded

1968 The Milwaukee Bucks are founded

1970 The Cleveland Cavaliers are founded

1971 The Milwaukee Bucks win the NBA title

1976 The Indiana Pacers join the NBA

1988 The New Orleans Hornets are founded as the Charlotte Hornets

1989 The Detroit Pistons win the first of their back-to-back NBA titles

1991 The Chicago Bulls win the first of six NBA titles

1995 The Toronto Raptors are founded

2002 The Hornets move to New Orleans

FOR MORE INFORMATION ABOUT THE CENTRAL DIVISION AND THE NBA

BOOKS

Aretha, David. *The Detroit Pistons Basketball Team.* Berkeley Heights, N.J.: Enslow Publishers, 2001.

Brunner, Conrad. *Boom Baby! The Sudden, Surprising Rise of the Indiana Pacers.* Indianapolis: Masters Press, 1994.

Doucette, Eddie. *The Milwaukee Bucks and the Remarkable Kareem Abdul-Jabbar.* Englewood Cliffs, N.J.: Prentice-Hall, 1974.

Frisch, Aaron. *The History of the Toronto Raptors.* Mankato, Minn.: Creative Education, 2002.

Nichols, John. *The History of the Atlanta Hawks.* Mankato, Minn.: Creative Education, 2001.

Nichols, John. *The History of Charlotte Hornets.* Mankato, Minn.: Creative Education, 2002.

Owens, Thomas S. *The Chicago Bulls Basketball Team.* Springfield, N.J.: Enslow Publishers, 1997.

ON THE WEB

Visit our home page for lots of links about Central Division teams:

http://www.childsworld.com/links.html

NOTE TO PARENTS, TEACHERS, AND LIBRARIANS: We routinely check our Web links to make sure they're safe, active sites—so encourage your readers to check them out!

INDEX

ABOUT THE AUTHOR

Robert E. Schnakenberg has written eight books on sports for young readers, including *Teammates: John Stockton and Karl Malone* and *Scottie Pippen: Reluctant Superstar.* He lives in Brooklyn, New York.